I0607044

P. Leo Haid

Major John Andre

An historical drama in five acts

P. Leo Haid

Major John Andre
An historical drama in five acts

ISBN/EAN: 9783741193224

Manufactured in Europe, USA, Canada, Australia, Japa

Cover: Foto ©Andreas Hilbeck / pixelio.de

Manufactured and distributed by brebook publishing software
(www.brebook.com)

P. Leo Haid

Major John Andre

Major John Andre:

AN HISTORICAL DRAMA

IN FIVE ACTS.

BY

P. LEO HAID, O. S. B.

*Director of the Senior Dramatic Association, St. Vincent
College, Westmoreland Co., Pa.*

———◆———

BALTIMORE:
PUBLISHED BY JOHN MURPHY & CO.
182 BALTIMORE STREET.
NEW YORK: CATHOLIC PUBLICATION SOCIETY.
1876.

RESPECTFULLY DEDICATED TO

"The Members of the Senior Dramatic Association,"

Of St. Vincent College,

IN PLEASANT RECOLLECTION

OF THE HOURS SPENT IN THEIR SOCIETY,

BY THE AUTHOR.

PREFACE.

The little drama, Major John Andre, was written during my leisure hours to assist in supplying a want, severely felt by those upon whom devolves the duty of selecting suitable plays for entertainments, where rule or custom forbids the introduction of *female* characters. It is not surprising that such plays are difficult to obtain, since the writer must dispense with a very important feature in representing real life; to this, pieces of this character, unless excellently played, will not experience a warm reception on any stage.

I endeavored to compensate for this necessary defect by an abundance of action, thus offering opportunities for the exercise of elocutionary powers, in nearly every circumstance requiring it. This will certainly receive the cordial approval of all interested in teaching or acquiring this important branch of a thorough education.

The plot upon which the drama rests, is historical, and needs no further comment. The latter half of the III., all of the IV. excepting the correspondence and some minor details, and part of the V. Acts are, of course, without any historical foundation. I had not the opportunity of obtaining copies of the original letters, documents, etc., required for the play, and can, therefore, only give what may have been their principal contents.

1*   v

I trust the play will be found free from anything objectionable even to the most sensitive. The virtues of patriotism, unswerving uprightness, filial affection, thoughtful care for the future, etc., are presented in a manner especially suited to make the proper impression on youthful hearts.

That it may do some little good, is the sincere desire of

THE WRITER.

St. Vincent College, *February 22, 1876.*

DRAMATIS PERSONÆ.

GEN. GEORGE WASHINGTON.
" GREENE.
" LAFAYETTE.
" ST. CLAIR.
" PUTNAM.
" HAMILTON.
" KNOX.
" STEUBEN.
" PARSONS.
COL. CLINTON.
" JAMESON.
MAJOR TALMAGE.
PAULDING,
VAN WERT, } Andre's Capturers.
WILLIAMS,
SIR HENRY CLINTON.
MAJOR JOHN ANDRE, the Spy.
JOHN ANDRE, SR., Major Andre's Father.
GEN. KNYPHAUSEN.
" ROBERTSON.
ADMIRAL GRAVES.
COL. CARLETON.
BENEDICT ARNOLD, the Traitor.
HEZEKIAH SMITH, a Tory.
PAGE TO SIR HENRY CLINTON.
GUARDS, &c.

Major John Andre.

Act I.

Scene I.—Hotel in New York City, A. D. 1780.

Sir Henry Clinton. (Alone.) More than five long
years have passed since first this cruel war began.
What noble blood has old England shed to conquer
and regain these rebellious Colonies! All in vain.
That traitor Washington, accursed his very name,
seems as one who knows no submission, feels no hard-
ships. The raw, undisciplined troops, too, fight like
tigers.

What has mighty England not done to quell this
rebellion? Thousands upon thousands have left the
nation's treasury; nearly every Protestant petty government in Europe, has sold its people to be butchered
by these rebels. Even the Indians, merciless bloodhounds though they are, have been let loose on these
traitors, but all for nought. And now whole Europe
seems aroused, yet no one power to aid England.
France, yes, papist France, dares openly espouse the
cause of our boorish foe. I always thought the Romish
Church hated *Republics,* hated liberty; I now see my
error. Her eldest daughter draws the sword for a
Republic! Catholic France in league with the Colonies! Ha, a strong enemy! How long will this bloody

9

strife continue? Here I am with England's choicest troops, straining every nerve to conquer whom? A mob of raw militia, with arms almost unfit for use, half clothed, half fed. What will I do when the chivalry of France assists them? Would I had never come to this nefarious nest of treason! Would I were again in merry England, then none could tempt me hither! But silence—some one comes. (Enter *Page*.)

Page. My Lord, strangers desire to speak to your Lordship.

Clinton. Bid them enter. (Exit *Page* with a low bow, which he always makes on entering or leaving the stage.) Who may they be? Ah! I almost forgot my engagements; Admiral Graves and Col. Carleton come. (Enter *Graves* and *Carleton* with military salute.) Welcome, my noble Sirs! Long have I expected you. Be seated. How fare our brothers in arms?

Graves. All is well, noble Lord. Admiral Rodney has quite baffled the French. The rebel Washington can scarcely move. All seems dark for the cause of the seditious Colonies. The soldiers from Jersey and Pennsylvania will disband unless they are paid within three days. The country seems tired of war, and can not long sustain its cruel privations. Soon the British Lion reigns here supreme. God hasten the moment!

Clinton. Well said, my noble Admiral, God hasten the wished-for hour! Yet me fears, we wish in vain. (Arising.) These rascally barbarians who call themselves soldiers, can well mutiny when no English are near; but no sooner do they hear the mother-country speak, when, as if possessed, they fly to arms, spurn our offers, and hang our envoys. Such are our foes! Rather than regain the King's favor, and serve him faithfully, they would live on a starving dog's rations, and brave, unclothed, the direst cold of northern winter! How fares L. Cornwallis?

Carleton. He could fare not better, noble Sir. All seems to fall before his arms, as fell the walls of Jerico before the trumpet's sound. Many and bloody were the battles, and bravely fought our valiant men. May England ever remember their deeds of dauntless might! Our foes, too, fight like lions. Pity it is, they spill their life's blood in a cause so bad. Yet, my Lord, their deeds of untold valor and heroic magnanimity, say much in their favor and go far to palliate their unjust cause. (*Clinton* gets impatient.) The fearless Baron de Kalb is no more; he fell leading on his men. His last words were those of one dying in freedom's cause. (*Clinton* give signs of displeasure.) The traitor and base rebel Sumter gives us much trouble. The devil seems to guide him. We find his movements swift and fearless. Though daily defeated and badly routed, he has killed more English soldiers than he ever had men in his rascally band. But now even he and Ben. Morgan seem discouraged. Gen. Gates has been completely routed, and could only muster one hundred and fifty men after a retreat of twenty miles. Both Carolinas and Georgia are totally in our power. Lord Cornwallis has declared martial law, and all who dare show resistance, are hanged like dogs. Soon none but loyal subjects shall tread Southern soil!

Clinton. Thanks for news so gladdening! May your efforts be crowned with every success, and

(Arising) perish all enemies of our royal master, the King!

Graves and Carleton. (Rising.) Long live George III.

Clinton. Amen! Here, good Carleton, take these papers to our noble brother, Lord Cornwallis, and with them, our sincerest good wishes. And you, dear Admiral, will hand these to Sir George Rodney. May he soon overcome, yes, destroy the papist French, now fostering, encouraging rebellion. Adieu!

Graves and Carleton. Adieu, your Lordship! When again we meet, may peace reign supreme! (Exeunt.)

Clinton. (Alone—bitterly.) Ah, yes! Well they speak of England's cause in the Colonies—yet I dread to think all their blood flows in vain. To tell the truth, I could well see Lord Cornwallis defeated. He is my rival. Well, well, I must assist him now, or I will be disgraced before the land. Alas! when victory does come, to come by other hands than mine. (Enter *Page.*) What now?

Page. My Lord, an old man craves an immediate audience.

Clinton. He may enter. (Exit *Page.*) Who may he be? Assassins swarm the country—I must be prepared. (Enter *H. Smith*, bowing slavishly—whining.)

Smith. Most noble Lord, England's bravest son.

Clinton. (Aside.) Ah, that slave must be a *tory;* none else could bow so low. Come to inform me of some secret design. (Aloud.) Thou art a faithful son of England, I presume!

Smith. The last drop of my heart's blood, I would gladly shed for England's cause.

Clinton. That is well. What news dost thou bring? Speak!

Smith. Long have I suffered and much endured for our good King George. My heart has often bled to see his Majesty's cause win so slowly. I have fought and bled, fearless and often, but to little purpose.

Clinton. (Interrupting) To the point, and praise not thyself so highly. (Sarcastically.) What new schemes can trouble *thy* brain?

Smith. Often when others slept I went from door to door, from place to place, to gather information for his Majesty's officers. Often did my disloyal countrymen point their fingers at me and say: "*See that scoundrel, he is a Tory.*"

Clinton. (Impatient.) Enough of this whining! To the point, I say, else I will point my sword at thee, may be closer than their fingers!

Smith. They not only *pointed* their fingers, but used them in robbing my house, maltreating my body, and—

Clinton. (Drawing his sword in anger.) By St. George, I'll rid them of thee! (Menacing with sword.)

Smith. (On his knees.) Oh! mercy, pity! Spare me; I'll tell you all.

Clinton. Be quick then, or I shall feed the dogs with thy carcass.

Smith. Here is a letter. (Rising.) It was sent you by Benedict Arnold who commands at West Point. (*Clinton* earnestly perusing the letter—betrays great interest—unmindful of *Smith.*) Yes, yes, I have suffered much! Everybody hates me. I work

2

day and night for England, and am paid so little;
they will not even listen to my complaints. (Approach-
ing *Clinton*.) O, good Lord! I have so much to tell
you. Please listen to me.

Clinton. You here yet? Take that and begone!
(Throws a purse upon the floor.)

Smith. (Eagerly clutching the money, on his knees.)
Oh, thanks, thanks! (Hurries off like a miser.)

Clinton. Yes, 'tis money these fellows want. But
let me see, this letter. I can scarcely believe my eyes.
Offers to surrender West Point, and all the forts which
so proudly protect the Hudson! It cannot be! Benedict Arnold is bad, but not *so bad*. I must call my
generals. Ho! (Enter *Page*.) Tell Generals Knyphausen and Robertson I would see them here at once.
(Exit.) Robertson knows Arnold's hand—he will
dispel every doubt.

SCENE II.

(Enter *Knyphausen* and *Robertson*.)

Both. My Lord, you sent for us.

Clinton. For business most extraordinary; General
Robertson, read this letter.

Robertson. (Reading aloud.)

WEST POINT, *Aug.* 10, 1780.

My Lord:—Be not surprised at receiving a note
from me. My wrongs are such that they must be
redressed. For years I led parts of the Colonial army,
and nearly always to victory, and yet my services are
undervalued. I am severely pressed by pecuniary

obligations, and the Colonial currency is little better than paper. I clearly see our efforts against England are vain. And now, as a last resort, our government has betrayed us into the hands of Romish France; this decides my course. I am prepared to enter into negotiations for the surrender of all posts under my command. General Washington will, within a few weeks, visit the French, just landed in Rhode Island; the command will then devolve on me. Send a trusty man to meet me at Hezekiah Smith's house, opposite West Point, on the Hudson.

Your obedient servant,

BENEDICT ARNOLD.

To SIR HENRY CLINTON, *New York.*

Knyphausen. (Blustering.) Long live George III! We will get you now, you rebellious scoundrels!

Clinton. But hold! Robertson, you know Arnold's hand. Is this his writing?

Robertson. Most assuredly, Sir! Every letter is his own.

Knyp. (Boisterously.) Hurrah for old England! Down with the rebels! Ah! traitor Washington, you have given us much trouble, but we have you now. *American Fabius* they call you; soon your carcass will be dangling from the gallows!

Robertson. Indeed, I am pleased. This will end the war. Peace again will reign and (with bitterness) Americans, you shall be *slaves* to England. Ah, yes! we will see your chains are heavy and well put on. You fought for *Liberty*, you said; the clanking of your chains shall resound over this broad land and make it the home of *slaves!* And the papist French, ha, how nicely they were duped!

Clinton. Yes, truly, this is a glorious day! Americans crushed, independence a dream! France, thou wilt now get thy share of war. England shall pay thee back, thou treacherous home of papist slaves!

Knyp. Marry, indeed, the sky is bright. Let's to work. Who shall be the trusty messenger?

Robertson. (Drawing back.) I would gladly offer my services, but cannot well leave my division of the army. (Aside.) In truth, 'tis too dangerous for my taste.

Knyp. I cannot leave my daring Hessians.

Clinton. (Aside.) I see both scent the danger. (Aloud.) Robertson, see if Major Andre is at home. (Exit.) I know Andre is brave; he loves adventure, and will gladly stake his liberty, yes, his life, on the success of a plan so decisive. (Enter *Andre.*)

Andre. Noble Lord, you called for me.

Clinton. I did. Read this letter. (*Andre* reads.)

Andre. I understand. You want a man to play the spy; a man who fears no danger in his country's cause. May I offer myself?

Knyp. How brave, how noble! You will write your name in golden letters on your country's gratitude. (Aside—slyly.) I would rather not have mine there under given circumstances.

Clinton. Noble Andre, I expected no less from you; you were always fearless. But the task is a dangerous one. Your good old father might censure my choice.

Andre. My father will not blame me when I act for my country.

Clinton. You are young—life's morn just begun. 'Tis but just you should know all. If you are arrested in this business, your life is forfeited. The spy's doom is the gallows. Consider well.

Andre. I have considered; I know they will hang me, if they lay their hands upon me. I know I will then die a felon's death, but this does not change my resolution. Lord Clinton, I am ready.

Clinton. Brave youth, I accept your offer. But be careful. Let every precaution be taken to evade capture. I will send the "Vulture" to conduct you within the Colonial lines, where Arnold meets you. Be prepared at seven to-night. Now go; meet me here at six, when I will give you all necessary papers. (Exit *Andre.*) Robertson, you shall command the "Vulture." Use every means to aid this plot.

Robertson. Most gladly, my Lord. (Exit.)

Clinton. And you General, hasten to your command. Hold it in readiness to move at a moment's notice.

Knyp. I will, my Lord. How joyfully will I retrieve the Hessian disgrace at Trenton! (Exit.)

Clinton. How advantageous for England this day's work! If by arms we succeed not, by treachery *thy own son* lays thee prostrate at our feet. But I must away, and prepare all necessary documents for the immortal Andre. How glad (gleefully) Lord Germain will be when he hears of this new scheme! (Exit R.)

Andre. (Enter L.) He is gone! Oh, how strange the feeling which overcomes me! I am sorry I accepted an office so dangerous, not that I fear the danger, but because I now see "*Honor*" has no part
2*

therein. But no! Do I not act for my native land, the dear land of my birth? Yes, all for England!— yet, to be a spy is dishonorable. Can England require *dishonor* to further her cause? Oh, dreadful cruel doubt! It is too late; I *must* go on! England, England, what a sacrifice I make for thee!

(*Curtain.*)

Act II.

SCENE I.—*Smith's House,—poorly furnished.*

(Enter R. *Williams* rather ragged, but an honest and good-natured Irishman. May assume the Irish dialect, so-called, making the appropriate changes in the wording of the sentences.)

Williams. (With his blackthorn.) Ha, here I am at last. This is the house of that sneaking tory Smith, bad 'cess to him. What joy it would give honest Paddy Williams to trounce the dirty sucker! The old miser would lick the feet of that bloody Orangeman George III, whom he adores as king. I'd lick his *royal highness* too, but it's with my cudgel I'd do it. Arrah, the mere thought of making the old scoundrel dance to the tune of my blackthorn, makes my heart jump! (Listens) Ha, what's that? (Steps heard.) Paddy, take care! I'll just hide here to hear what the old thief has to say. (Hides, menacing with blackthorn.)

Smith. (Enters, looking stealthily around.) I can scarcely be secure in my own house! Ha, ha! here's what I got for my letter! (Shows purse.) How heavy it is! Surely, that letter must have been very important. Why did I not open and read it, I might have received still more? This evening General Arnold comes with the man who arrived in the British ship to-day. What can the object of their meeting be? I must store away this treasure, then listen to the plans. (Exit.)

Williams. (Coming slowly from his hiding-place.) That was the tory Smith. How he hugged the money! The old miser would sell not only his country and liberty, but his black *soul* for *money*. But the old boy would give him little for that: begorra! he has it already. I hear horses coming; I will be gone, and call Paulding and Van Wert. Mr. Arnold, I don't trust you, and will keep an eye on your capers. (Exit as before.)

SCENE II.

(Enter *Arnold* and *Andre*, *Arnold* very cautiously leading the way; *Andre* in blue uniform.)

Arnold. Here my friend, be seated; I will lock every door. Now tell me quickly, what does Lord Clinton mean to do? Has he given you authority to complete the negotiations commenced?

Andre. Lord Clinton greets you in his, and in his country's name. He fully appreciates the importance of this affair. He knows it has cost you many sleepless nights to come to a decision so fatal to the Colonies, and so full of grand results for England. He knows too, your noble spirit would spurn what *honor* cannot claim for his own. Total hopelessness of the Colonial cause, and the desire of avoiding further bloodshed, alone, could induce your dauntless soul to take this step.

Arnold. (Confused.) I thank Lord Clinton for his noble thoughts and consoling words. (Impatiently.) But we must be quick. To the point. He knows my demands; does he grant them?

Andre. (Taking papers from his boots.) Here are papers; in them you will find all. Lest I should lose them, or they should fall into an enemy's hand, he gave me some verbal orders. You demand £10,000, and the office of Major General in his Majesty's army; the money he gladly grants,—the office he cannot. His commission forbids him giving any higher than that of Brigadier. Would you accept this in exchange?

Arnold. (Displeased.) I am a Major-General in the Colonial army, and might reasonably expect the same office in his Majesty's; yet, since Lord Clinton's power is limited, I will accept the other.

Andre. (Rising.) Receive Lord Clinton's thanks and mine. Here (giving papers) is your Commission; here (giving bank notes) are £5,000; the balance will be handed over as soon as your part of the contract is fulfilled.

Arnold. (Slowly receiving the bribes.) My thanks. (Handing papers.) Give these to Lord Clinton. He will find diagrams of the five forts, and the number of soldiers in each. Let the attack be made on the day appointed. But you must be fatigued. Go up stairs, you will find refreshments and all prepared. When rested, your horse awaits you. Go then in all haste and secrecy to the "Vulture." Now, adieu! I must return to my post.

Andre. Adieu! May no mishap come between our plans. I will hurry to refresh myself and return. Oh! I am so glad all goes so smoothly. Adieu. (Exit L.)

Arnold. (After some moments of deep thought, slowly pacing the stage.) Benedict Arnold, thou art a

Traitor! Thou hast sold thy honor, the blood and
freedom of thy countrymen for a handful of *Gold!*
Great Heavens! has it come to this? Did I imagine
when first I began my profligate life that it would end
in *treachery?* Arnold the *Traitor!* What a name!
And shall mine go down to posterity so? 'Traitor
branded on my forehead!—Could my gallant father see
me now, what would he say? Methinks his bones are
restless in the cold grave, to think his son, his once darling boy, has become the cruel betrayer of his people!
Arnold the *Traitor!* So the child, yet unborn, will
read in its country's history. Generations yet to come
will learn my name but to *curse* it as the cause of the
chains which shackle their freedom. Arnold the
Traitor! Is it for this thou didst fight and bleed so
long? Is it for this, thou for five long years didst
lead thy countrymen, and see them die with a smile
upon their lips, because it was for liberty? Is it for
this thou didst cross the country, enter Canada, and
brave the once hated British,—mock at its northern
cold? Ah! how my soldiers, ill-clothed and starving
as they were, would greet my hopeful glance! How
they once cheered for Benedict Arnold! Now they
will curse me, execrate the memory of their country's
betrayer! But hold! The deed is not yet done; I
have still time to retrace my steps—Andre is yet here.
I will go to him, cast the money at his feet, regain my
papers and my honor! (As if about to go—stops—
returns.) Yet, how can I recall my plighted word?
How pay my debts, how continue my profligate life,
without English money? No! I cannot relinquish
my mode of life! Have I not been abased by Con-

gress? Have not others been preferred to me? Have they not, a few months ago, removed me from my comfortable quarters in Philadelphia, and put me on those hills? Yes, my actions, my deeds of valor, my genius, have been undervalued. I have suffered insults from those ruffians! (Furiously.) *Money* and *Revenge!* Let others curse me, let future generations spit upon my memory, I will have money! I cannot change my manner of living. They may call it the price of blood, of liberty; I call it the means of pleasure. Arnold, thou must go on—it is too late! *Money* and *Revenge!* Listen! I have delayed too long. I must away! (Exit L.)

SCENE II.— *Woods—on* L. *Smith's house.*

(Enter R., *Williams, Paulding* and *Van Wert,* poorly clad—torn boots—muskets in readiness.)

Williams. (Slyly.) Here we are at last, boys. Yonder, (pointing L.,) is that serpent Smith's house. I'll bet my head he is a bloody Tory, and is doing everything to injure the good cause. I'll just eye around a little. (Goes out L.)

Paulding. Indeed, I saw that British ship come near, and Arnold sent a small boat to meet that young stranger. I fear there is danger.

Van Wert. (May assume the German dialect under the same conditions prescribed for *Williams.*) Yes, that Arnold seems to be a villain. He goes about with his eyes wide open, and looks so scared that something must be wrong. If I could only lay my hands on one of those sneaking red-coats, certainly, it would be the worse for him.

Williams. (Re-entering.) Upon my soul, I can find nothing. The house yonder is as quiet as midnight. What will we do?

Paulding. We *must* ferret out this thing and remain here. To pass the time, come let us have a game at cards. Williams, you watch that side, (pointing R.,) Van Wert will look to this.

Van Wert. Ha, ha! Very good! We will play "Seven up."

Williams. No, my friend, "Forty-five" is just the thing.

Paulding. I see you can't agree. I will offer a compromise. Euchre is a game all can play.

Will. and V. Wert. Yes, yes! We will play euchre. (Sitting down—*Van Wert* facing L., *Williams* R., and *Paulding* audience.)

Paulding. Watch your posts, and don't let the game engage you too much. Who turns up? (They arrange matters, and play one round, occasionally looking about.)

Van Wert. (Pointing L.) What's that? A man on horseback! See, he comes this way! (All three rise—walk towards L.)

Williams. That, upon my honor, is the young fellow who came from the English ship last evening.

Paulding. (Meeting *Andre* at L. entrance.) Stranger, dismount. Where may you come from?

Andre. Whither do you belong?

Van Wert. Below, if it pleases you.

Williams. Yes, your honor, we belong to the lower party.

Andre. I have that honor too. Let me pass: I have something of importance to attend to.

Paulding. But you have not told us where you are going.

Andre. You are faithful servants of his Britannic Majesty. I am for New York to see Sir Henry Clinton.

Williams. Ha, ha! There you are mistaken! Blast his Britannic Majesty! I'm a true son of America, and so are my comrades.

Andre. (Aside.) A nice mess I have gotten myself into. (Aloud.) I am an envoy; here are my papers from General Arnold; this is a free pass. Let me go, or you will frustrate the General's plans.

Williams. As we don't know what those plans you speak of are, we would like to hear them.

Andre. (Angrily.) You look like highway robbers! Let me pass, I say, or Arnold's vengeance will fall upon you.

Van Wert. You call *us* robbers! You murdering Englishmen stole what we had, and now you call *us* robbers. I say as long as Van Wert has blood in his veins, you shall not pass. (Presents musket.)

Paulding. Spies, good sir, swarm the country. Bad men are more than plenty, and you may be one of them.

Williams. Yes, my darling, let me search you, and if all is well, you may pass.

Andre. (Distressed—aside.) These ragged vagabonds are shrewder than I took them for. I will bribe them.

Van Wert. What's that you say? Do you think that, because our clothes are tattered, we have not good manners? Speak loud!

3

Andre. (Aside.) Accursed thieves! (Aloud.) You are in want. Your country cannot require so much from you. Here is a purse of *Gold*—take and divide it. (To *Paulding.*)

Paulding. (Stepping back.) Man! how dare you offer me gold? Think you I am a robber? And, if you are guilty, think you I would let you pass for a few gold pieces? You little know the patriot's heart. You say I am in want; only too true. But what is the cause? A few years ago, our fields were gold with ripening grain; our fruitful valleys teemed with vegetation; and herds of cattle roamed, where now all is waste and ruin. Who caused this dreadful change? Who substituted rags for comfortable clothing? Our feet are almost bare and long since frozen. Who is to blame for all this suffering, all this untold misery? (Furiously.) England! That base, blood-thirsty, godless rascal, who calls himself George III. Yes, an English Parliament, subservient and debased, saw our rich lands and blooming valleys. Its own wars had emptied the treasury. It must be replenished, and without permitting us to be represented, you taxed us cruelly! We resisted! You are sent over to conquer, to crush us! Your government has let loose the merciless Indian, that firebrand of hell, upon us! Behold the Wyoming Valley! A blackened desert. The wails of helpless children still resound in my ears. O Heavens! I saw the child torn from its weeping, heart-broken mother, and *butchered* midst the hideous laugh of the Indian bloodhound! The mother drowned in the warm blood of her child! The helpless old man, with the snow of eighty winters upon his venerable head, scalped, butchered—his gray hair borne away as a trophy of victory! All this cruel England has done! You bid me now forget these wrongs for *gold!* Man, man! I am tempted to smatter thy brains upon the ground! (Raises his musket to strike.)

Williams. Oh, Paulding, darling, be easy with him now! (Holding his arm.) (To *Andre.*) You bloody Saccenach, you deserve to have your brains smashed out, but I pity your ignorance. What, you want Pat. Williams to let you pass for gold! If you are *good*, I'll let you go for *nothing;* if bad, no *price* can buy you. Friend Paulding has just told you why Americans owe you a debt of vengeance. My blood boils in my veins when I think of what you have done to Ireland. Ah! you English tyrants have changed the fair land of the Shamrock, into a land of paupers. You have robbed us of land, liberty, and would take our faith, but to do this, you must take the Irish heart. You drove us from the Green Isle like slaves, like dogs, and when we found a free home here, you would again enchain us. How many of my brave countrymen have died fighting for the British flag, and yet you tread them in the dust. The honest name of *Irishman* is a term of infamy with you. You would flatter me now to gain your point; but remember I have an Irish heart, and *that* heart is honest. I am an exile, you are my persecutor. You drove me from the land I love, then offer me money to sell the only thing I have left—my *honesty.* Take away that purse, or my stick shall make an acquaintance with your artful head!

Andre. (To *Van Wert.*) Here, friend, you take the money. I mean well with you all, and would not ask you to barter your honesty.

Van Wert. (Laughing scornfully.) Oh, you serpent-tongued rogue! Do not ask us to sell our honor! You are a worthy son of England. Not a small Protestant country in whole Europe, but you English scoundrels bought some of its people for foreign, unjust wars. Not the common people; no, they are good; but that Nation's curse, you call them "*Noblemen*" ! That proud, arrogant, haughty, lazy set, who live and thrive and fatten, on the poor, honest citizen's labor, sweat and blood! Look at my own fair land, Hessia! That blood sucker, the Landgrave, has sold hundreds of my countrymen to bloated England, to be butchered in a foreign land, cursed by its inhabitants, and scorned by those they served! Yes, just stare at me! I was cruelly kidnapped from my poor family, my weeping wife and hapless children. I succeeded in deserting your infamous cause, and had my dear ones in this free land, when you enemies of mankind, like the frost which withers the new-born plant, nipped my happiness in its very bud. My house is burnt, my family scattered, I know not whither! *Now* you offer me gold! Shame should make your face as scarlet!

Andre. (Aside.) What can I do? Heavens, they will discover all. (Takes out his watch and offers. Aloud.) Here is the purse; my watch I freely add. My good King will not forget this favor. He will make you rich and happy. Your families he will collect, and give them more than human heart can desire. My word as an officer of the royal army on what I promise.

Paulding. Keep your money, watch, and promises! We must know more about you. Come, we will search him.

Williams. True as you are living, I will lend a willing hand.

Van Wert. Come young man, do not force us to use violence.

Andre. (Proudly replacing money, &c., draws his sword.) Search me! No, you groveling, dirty wretches, never! Back, or I shall let day-light through your bodies!——

Paulding. Men, surround him! Shoot him as you would a dog, if he dare resist. Forward!

Van Wert. Young man, we are three to one. Submit!

Andre. (Haughtily.) Never! (At *Williams.*) Die, you papist dog!

Williams. (Parries the thrust with his blackthorn.) Not so fast! (Fencing—to others.) Don't shoot! I'll give the fellow a taste of what I learned at Donnybrook fair. (Fences—moves quickly, evading *Andre's* blows.) I'll not hurt you, only clip (strikes him on the hand) your fingers. (Rushes at him, throwing him to the ground.)

Andre. (Drops sword when struck by *Williams.*) Accursed, low-bred scoundrel! (Struggling violently.)

Williams. Be easy, my dear! Don't kick so, you'll spoil your boots. Be quick men, search him. (Search.)

Andre. Oh! you downright scoundrels! An English officer thus maltreated! Vengeance, dark vengeance on your heads!

Paulding. We can find nothing. We have wronged him, perhaps.

3*

Williams. (Letting him partially up.)   I meant no harm.   If he had nothing, why refuse to let us search him?

Van Wert.   Do not let him go; pull off his boots! (*Andre* struggling more violently, using complimentary terms.   They find the papers.)

Paulding.   (Reading — after a moment's pause.) Great Heavens!   What a dreadful plot!   Gustavus! Who may that be?   Arrangements for the surrender of West Point!

Will. and V. Wert.   Oh, terrible!   You black-hearted spy!

Paulding.   Bind him!

Williams.   In my belt you will find a rope.   Give it here.   (They bind him.)

Andre.   Alas!   I am lost.   Friends, have pity on me.   Take me to General Arnold's headquarters.

Williams.   Arnold, sir?   Perhaps he is the traitor! Nice job to take you to the man who caused you this fearful trial.   No, no!   Van Wert, keep hold of this man; I will call Colonel Jameson and Major Talmage. Hold him fast, I will soon be back.   (Exit R.)

Van Wert.   Young man, your life is in the greatest peril.   Confess all, and tell us Gustavus' real name, and you may yet be saved.

Andre.   I know what fate awaits me.   Your treatment has been such, I can hope for nothing from you.

Van Wert.   Nothing dishonorable, but—(Interrupted by *Williams* calling, from without.)

Williams.   Here you are Colonel and Major.   By all that's good we want you. (Entering.) See here this spalpeen!   He is a spy.

Jameson. (Surprised.) What is all this uproar? Why did you bind this man? What is his name? Who is he?

Paulding. (Who has thoroughly examined the papers in the meantime.) Blackest treason! Here a description of West Point; diagrams of the forts; number of men in each—all truly given. The letters are entrusted to the care of Anderson by Gustavus. This must be Anderson; who may Gustavus be?

Talmage. (Taking papers from *Paulding.*) Can this be true? Yes, every word! Great Heavens! A *traitor* in our ranks and at headquarters too!

Jameson. Unbind the prisoner! Now, sir, what mystery is this?

Andre. I will say nothing to you. Take me to the headquarters of General Arnold, and I will divulge all.

Talmage. (Who has been reading.) Oh, what a fiendish plot! (*Jameson* takes *Andre* aside.)

Van Wert. Such downright roguery! When they fail in fair and open battle, intrigue, devilish plans must help them!

Williams. I see it all now; how fortunate for the patriot cause, we watched this sly rascal.

Jameson. Major, take these men away; I will conduct this young Englishman to a safe place.

Paulding. Whither will you take him?

Jameson. No cause of yours! I command here!

Paulding. But it is! We captured this spy, and have a right to see that he is put into proper hands.

Jameson. (Angrily.) Are *mine* not proper?

Williams. Sure they are, sir, but I had the greatest bother capturing this rascal, and will know where he is going before he leaves this place.

Talmage. Yes, Colonel, these men have acted nobly —they spurned his bribes, and manfully did their duty. Tell them whither you wish to lead the prisoner.

Jameson. Well, if you must know, to General Arnold's tent.

Williams. Then you will have to pass over my dead body!

Jameson. Dare you oppose my wishes?

Van Wert. Williams is right. I too will help to hang him here and now, rather than that he should be sent to Arnold.

Talmage. Colonel Jameson, I can scarcely comprehend you. These men are justified, from what they saw and heard, in suspecting that General. Do not force your opinion upon them. I protest with them!

Paulding. He shall not be sent to Arnold. I will remain at his side, and the moment any such attempt is made, I will oppose it even at the risk of my life.

Williams. (Losing patience.) Colonel Jameson, if you do not desist, I will knock his brains out, and end the whole affair!

Andre. Colonel, I see it cannot be done; I merely desired to see the General, as I hold passports from him. Permit me to send this note; it will explain my situation.

Jameson. You cannot object to that! (To *Andre.*) I will carry your note in person; give it to me. (To *Talmage.*) Major, I entrust this man to you, and will expect to receive him at your hands. Van Wert and

Paulding will accompany you to Morristown. I meet you there this evening. Go! (Exeunt. *Williams* secretes himself.) This is a dark mystery. I pity the young Englishman, and would gladly set him free, but I must be cautious; that wild Irishman seems bent on his destruction. I will hurry this note to Arnold. (Exit L.)

Williams. (Enters R., cautiously.) Colonel Jameson, can you be in league with this spy! I am bent on this fellow's destruction, and on yours too, if you are not very careful. I must now hurry off to meet Washington, who, with his staff, will pass within half a mile this evening. I will tell him all. Blast the traitors and spies! If I meet that Arnold, I'll give him a remembrance. But, I must be off. (Exit R.)

SCENE III.—*Interior of Smith's house.*

Smith. (Frightened.) I thought I heard some one speak. Alas! what a day of troubles! Since early morning I have been busily engaged working against these rebels. Everywhere I come, fingers are pointed at me, and I can plainly read the unuttered curse on angry faces. This evening everybody seems more than usually excited. From lips to lips, like the fire on our Western prairies, fly the words : " Treason, treachery, traitor." I thought I heard Arnold's name. Oh! if that young Englishman should have fallen into their hands! My blood freezes in my veins to think what an awful fate would await him and (whining) *me* too. But see! here comes General Arnold, riding like a mad man !

Arnold. (Somewhat intoxicated.) Ah! Smith, you look rather down-hearted. What's happened? For me, the day has been a jolly one! Plenty of money and plenty of wine. I've played with unusual success. Then, all is in readiness; the troops are stationed so, that resistance will be impossible. To-morrow Lord Clinton attacks the forts, and captures them too! Any old Rye here? Why, man, you look as dreary as a night owl! What's the matter?

Smith. I have heard rumors of *Treason* on every side this evening. The people are furious, and swear they will hang every traitor and Tory they can lay their hands on. Have you noticed nothing?

Arnold. You're a bird of evil omen, Smith. But, ho! I did receive a note from Colonel Jameson. I was too busy to read it. Let me see. (Opens the note —gasping.) From Major Andre! In ciphers! By all that's evil Andre is captured! My papers in the capturers' hands! I am lost! Smith! quick, saddle my swiftest horse, away! (Exit frightened.) Oh, what a misfortune! I'm detected! If they can lay hold on me, the infuriated people will tear me to pieces! I *must* save myself! Already the fruits of treason ripen. Here they will search first! I must bribe Smith. Let that cursed Tory perish, I must be saved!

Smith. (Re-entering—whining.) The horse is ready!

Arnold. Good, my faithful friend. Here is a purse; keep it. Remain here, and if any one asks for me, say I am gone. They may find me at West Point.

Smith. (Clutching money—afraid and trembling.) But, but—they will take me—hang me! I cannot do what you require! They will think I'm in league with you. I too must go!

Arnold. (Holding him.) No, you shall not go! Remain here you must! If you dare not speak, let on you're deaf and dumb! This you can do. Detain them as long as you can; I will soon be beyond their reach. I'll reward you richly. (Gives more money.)

Smith. (Grasping the money.) I'll do the best I can.

Arnold. Thanks, my friend! Here, take this. (Gives money.) Mind, you can neither hear nor speak. I am off. (Exit.)

Smith. What will become of me? I hope none of them will know me. More *money!* That is the *only* thing I would risk my life for! (Frightened.) I hear the galloping of horses! I will get into that corner. (Goes to the left corner—sits, holding his head in his hands.)

Washington. (From without—loud.) This is the house, men! Surround it, and let no man pass!

Putnam. (From without—very angrily.) I will shoot the first treacherous rascal I can find!

SCENE IV.

(Enter *Washington* and *Lafayette* R.—hurriedly.)

Wash. The room is empty! The bird has flown! Oh, such base treachery!

Lafayette. Has it come to this? My goodness, what a dreadful plot!

Putnam. (Entering L.—stumbling over *Smith.*) No one in the room! Who's this? It must be a cursed Tory, no patriot could cower so dog-like. (Kicking.) Wake up, you sneaking scoundrel!

Wash. and Laf. Who may it be? Speak, man!

Putnam. He is a knave or a fool! (Yelling.) Do you hear? The vagabond seems to be deaf. Wake up, or I'll blow your brains out. (Shoots pistol over his head—*Smith* trembles.) Ha, you seem to smell the smoke if you don't hear the sound!

Wash. Have mercy, General! perhaps the man is deaf and dumb. (Enter *Williams*, R.)

Williams. The rascal is neither the one nor t'other!

Putnam. Do you know him? (*Williams* winks knowingly.)

Putnam. (Exasperated.) You infernal scoundrel, are you trying to play on us? (Catches *Smith*—takes him to the front—drawing his sword.) I'll cut out your slavish tongue if you do not speak!

Smith. (Very much frightened.) I can't speak!

Putnam. You can't! Then blast your lying mouth, what evil spirit spoke out of you just now?

Lafayette. Man, you are detected. At the peril of your life answer every question.

Wash. Yes, answer! I thought the General was cruel, but I beg his pardon; he was right.

Putnam. I know your noble heart, Washington. Such downright meanness is foreign even to your thoughts. But I know these knaves better. (Angrily to *Smith.*) Speak, man, and speak the truth, or I'll brain you!

Wash. What is your name?

Smith. (Very slavishly.) May it please your Lordship, Smith.

Putnam. Ha, ha, ha! The slave thinks he is
speaking to some English Turk who calls himself
Lord! Don't say *Lordship* again, or I'll slice your
base tongue!

Wash. Was General Arnold here this evening?

Smith. My Lord—

Putnam. Scoundrel, don't *Lord* him!

Smith. May it please your—(*Putnam* threatens,)
Generalship, I don't like to tell!

Lafayette. So he was here; when did he leave?

Smith. I have no clock, you see—

Putnam. No such answers! About the time, quick!

Smith. Two hours.

Wash. Which way did he go?

Smith. I did not see, but he said he was going to
West Point.

Lafayette. General, he told this man a lie. (Enter
Greene, Hamilton and *Knox.*)

Greene. No one has left the premises, as we surrounded the house completely; he must have gone
before.

Knox. Most certainly, sir! A boy I met told me
he had seen a man in blue uniform ride towards New
York.

Hamilton. General, it was Arnold! He must have
heard of his detection. Great Heavens! There must
be more traitors here than one! Who is this fellow?

Putnam. A Tory, by his servile speech! Rascal,
did Arnold know he was detected?

Smith. He had a note!

4

Lafayette. Yes, here it is; he dropped it. In ciphers! (All crowd around *Hamilton, Putnam* forgetting *Smith,* who sneaks away—when about to rush out, is caught by *Williams.*)

Williams. (Collaring him.) Not so fast, darling! The gentlemen are not through with you yet!

Hamilton. I know these ciphers.—" I'm captured— papers discovered—save yourself. Anderson."

Lafayette. Ah, poor fellow, you are too honest to be a spy!

Wash. No time to lose. Putnam and Knox follow Arnold! He has gone to New York; bring him back dead or alive!

Putnam and Knox. We will, General. Woe to his treacherous heart if we lay hands on him! (Exeunt hurriedly, L.)

Wash. General Greene, off to Morristown! Chain the spy! Call a meeting of officers to decide his fate.

Greene. I will attend to all. (Exit R.)

Wash. We will go to West Point. My God! may it not be too late!

Hamilton. Be calm, dear sir! We could hear the noise of battle were one in progress. Oh, such diabolical treachery.

Lafayette. True, man's mind could conceive nothing more abominable!

Wash. All was progressing so fairly: Our troops reclothed and armed, and in good spirits; our faithful allies, your brave countrymen, whom we have just seen so willing, so able to assist us in striking off the tyrant's chains. I shall ever love sunny France and her brave people! May God preserve them! Most truly the day will come when France too, will no longer acknowledge King nor Emperor! But we must away—Lafayette, you to the eastern end; Hamilton, to the western; I will to the centre. (Going.)

Williams. Beg your pardon! (Stops him.) But what of Smith?

Wash. Ah, good, noble-hearted son of Ireland, I had almost forgotten! I leave him to you; guard him, and take him to Morristown. (Exit.)

Williams. Come along, you old thief, I'll store you safely away. (Exeunt— *Williams* encouraging *Smith's* progress with his cudgel.)

(*Curtain.*)

N. B —Where the arrangements of the stage do not admit of quick changes of the scenery, etc., the second scene of this act will take better if played in Smith's house, like the first. By changing a few words, this may be done as far as the actors are concerned.

ACT III.

ANDRE'S TRIAL.

SCENE I.—*A large Hall—table in back centre. Arranged in a semi-circle, Generals Greene, Lafayette, St. Clair, Putnam, Knox, Steuben, Parsons and Col. Clinton. General Greene presiding.*

Greene. Fellow Patriots! For the first time, since the beginning of the war for Independence, we are assembled to perform a duty so painful. One of our Generals, a man beloved of all, brave and fearless, gifted with uncommon genius and military abilities, has sold his name, his honor, and almost the blood of his countrymen and their hope of freedom, for filthy lucre!

All. (Enraged.) A country's curse upon his memory!

Greene. Benedict Arnold has become a *Traitor!* He wanted money to continue his wicked career, so lately commenced, and determined to surrender all posts under his command to Sir Henry Clinton. Major John Andre was deputed by the British General to arrange the terms, to receive and sign all necessary papers to complete this hellish contract. All was done, and Andre was again on his way to New York, when he met our three brave co-patriots, Paulding, Van Wert, and Williams. When closely pressed, he endeavored to bribe them to regain his liberty. May Americans yet unborn remember their unselfish devotion to duty! He failed, was searched, papers implicating him in a plot too dark for English words to

name, were found in his boots. He is now in chains.
We are called upon to decide his fate. You all know
that death, an ignomenious death too, rewards the spy.
Let us then coolly, for we sit as judges, examine every
circumstance, and give our verdict as conscience may
dictate. Shall I call the prisoner?

Putnam. Much reason why! Were not the papers
found on his person? Has not Arnold, the accursed
traitor, escaped in hot haste to Clinton's lines? What
more would you have? It is clear as noon-day, Andre
is **a spy,** and as such must *die!*

Lafayette. General Putnam! I know your honesty
of purpose. Circumstances, indeed, are strongly against
the young Englishman, yet he may have something to
say which will at least palliate his dark deed.

St. Clair. No man should be condemned without a
hearing!

Knox. True, but did our poor fellows always fare
so at British hands? No! like dogs they were hanged!
Not spies either! Ask bold Sumter where many of
his bravest soldiers are. He will point you to the
palmetto, and bid you count their bleached *skeletons*
dangling from the branches! *They* died without a
hearing; why should we be so merciful to British
spies?

Parsons. British injustice and cruelty should not
make *us* forget that we are both *just* and *merciful.*

Steuben. Well said! English barbarity deserves
punishment, not imitation. I move the prisoner be
brought before this commission.

Col. Clinton. I agree with General Steuben. I
second the motion.

4*

Putnam. I see the sentiment of the majority is against me. I withdraw my objection.

Knox. And I mine. Perhaps it is better so. If the young Englishman is upright, his own confession will condemn him; if not, the crime is easily proved.

Greene. Guards! bring in the prisoner. Shall we give him an advocate?

Lafayette. Certainly, if he desires his services.

Putnam. (Sarcastically.) He should send for Arnold. (Enter *Andre,* accompanied by *Jameson* and *Talmage.*)

Greene. (Writing.) Prisoner, what is your name?

Andre. My name is John Andre. I am an officer in his Majesty's army, Adjutant-General to Sir Henry Clinton.

Knox. A few weeks ago, you were known as "Anderson." You changed your name then.

Andre. My name is Andre; Anderson was but adopted.

Greene. Major Andre, it is not unknown to you why you are called upon to appear before us to-day. You are accused of a crime, which, unless disproved, will condemn you to death. Have you selected, or do you desire an advocate to plead your cause?

Andre. I have not selected, nor do I desire one. I will speak for myself. The papers found upon my person, I see before you. I have no desire to deny what they speak against me. I did negotiate with General Arnold for the surrender of West Point and surrounding forts; I did so in the interest of the English government. I did not suppose my action was against the laws of war, or dishonest. I knew that death would follow my detection, but that a brave soldier fears not.

Putnam. Who proposed this line of conduct to you? Was it not Sir Henry Clinton?

Andre. I am here to speak of my own actions, not those of others.

Putnam. Young man, you are too good to be under such evil influences as George's officers in America.

Andre. You are a blunt soldier and speak freely; but I cannot accept the compliment.

Greene. Then you deny nothing. Young man, remember your own confession is your death-warrant!

Andre. I will not tell a wilful falsehood, but would bid you consider well what the consequences of my death will be. Lord Clinton holds many of your officers; Lord Cornwallis too. They are, both told me, hostages for my safety. You imperil their lives by taking mine!

Putnam. (Angrily.) By my honor, and did not both hang Americans like dogs long ere this, without a trial, without a hearing too? Do these wretched tyrants hope to bind our hands by means so low? Let them dare hang but the least prisoner in their hands, and, as true as *I hate* England, I shall hang every prisoner, great or small, that falls into my hands!

Greene. The only man who can save your life is Arnold. If Clinton delivers that traitor into our power, you are free. This he has refused to do, and you must die, unless you can move him to grant our demands.

Andre. No, this I cannot ask of Lord Clinton. If there is no other means of saving my life, I can only request a soldier's death.

Knox. General Greene, we know enough. Let the prisoner be returned to his cell.

Greene. Major Andre, is this all you have to say?

Andre. All just now. Only in giving your verdict, remember what I have said.

Greene. Guards, return him to the prison. (Exeunt.) Now, gentlemen, what verdict shall we give?

Lafayette. The young man acknowledges his dark deed. I pity his youth, and can but blame Lord Clinton for enticing one so young, so brave, to perform a deed so bad. My voice, though it makes my heart bleed, is for his *death.*

St. Clair. I too must say the same—he must die!

Putnam. Certainly, he must die!

Greene. Is this sentiment unanimous?

All. (Rising.) It is. Let him die!

Greene. (Deeply moved.) May God have mercy on his soul!

Knox. A spy's doom is the *gallows.* A soldier's death he cannot receive.

Putnam. Let sentiment be sentiment; he *must be hanged!* (Enter *Washington* and *Hamilton.*)

All. (Rising.) Hail to our honored chief!

Wash. Thanks! What verdict have you given?

Greene. *Guilty.* His own confession demanded death.

Hamilton. Alas! poor young man, my heart bleeds for him!

Wash. *Justice* must have its course. I knew long since no jury could acquit him. The thought that he must die, has caused me many sorrowful hours. But duty to my country is paramount.

Greene. Here is the death-warrant. Your signature alone is wanting.

Wash. (In great agitation.) Is this your verdict? Must he die?

All. He has deserved death : let him die !

Wash. O, the fearful alternative! The disgrace and dishonor of the nation I have sworn to serve, or the *death* of one so young, so brave! But why do I falter? (Takes up the pen.) Duty marks out my path ! O Arnold! Traitor Arnold, his blood be upon *thy* head. (Signs.—Leaves the stage L.—Recalled by *Andre's* father.)

Scene II.

Father. (*Andre's* father rushes in R. wildly.) Where is my son, my darling boy ?

Wash. (Returning—faces him—mildly.) Good man, I have not seen you before; who are you ?

Father. A heart-broken old man ! I am Major Andre's father !

Hamilton. (Aside.) Alas, alas ! Old man, I pity you !

Father. Where is my boy? Does he still live? O tell me! I have crossed the stormy ocean to see, to speak to him. Am I too late? Where is my boy? (Looking wildly around.)

Wash. Calm yourself, my dear sir, your boy lives, but is in prison. (Aside.) Alas ! he soon must die!

Father. Thank God, he still lives! You will not put him to death! O speak! Tell me my son will soon be free !

Wash. (Sorrowfully.) Old man, it would be more than cruel to deceive you. Only one thing can save your son, and that—

Father. O tell me! Take my life! I am old, and gladly give it to save my son's!

Greene. This scene becomes too painful.

Wash. Your life, my dear old man, cannot save your son's.

Father. What then? If it is in man's power I will do it, and my thanks shall cease but with my breath!

Putnam. It is in man's power, but both are worse than tigers. Arnold the traitor must be surrendered!

Father. And does he refuse? will not Clinton force him?

Wash. Arnold refuses, and Clinton encourages his refusal!

Father. O base demons! First you entice away my child, then refuse to save him! Oh! how black your hearts!

Wash. This refusal *forces* us to put to death Major Andre.

Father. (Wildly.) What! kill my boy! O kind sirs! it was not his crime! He was misled! He is so young, not yet twenty-four. Oh! have mercy on him and me. Spare, do spare my child!

Wash. And sacrifice our country! Old man, to spare your son would require us to submit to disgrace, dishonor. Spies deserve death; he confesses he is a spy and must therefore die!

Father. (Kneeling.) Good sir, kind sir, take back that word! He must not die! Look upon me! I am old, my hair is silvered with the snows of eighty winters! He is the child of my old age! Oh! pity, mercy! Oh! listen to my words; break not a fond

father's heart! Save, oh! save my boy! Kind sirs,
do spare my child!

Lafayette. Good Heavens! this sight brings tears
to my eyes. I would rather face ten thousand English soldiers than this poor old man. Washington,
end it!

Wash. (In broken voice.) Pray, old man, leave
off thy prayers. My life I would gladly give to save
your son, but not my and my country's honor. Arise!

Father. Have you hearts of stone? If my words
move you not, listen to the prayers of a loving mother.
Beyond the billowy sea her hands are lifted up to
Heaven for mercy! Sisters and brothers join with
her. The same prayer on every lip—the same deep
sorrow chokes every voice! By the love you bore
your own dear mothers; by everything that is good
and holy in this world, I beg you, pray you, spare, oh!
do spare my son!

Putnam. (Greatly moved.) This is terrible—it is
unbearable! Old man, arise! If you desire our lives,
mine is at your disposal; but our country, we cannot
shame!

Wash. It must be ended; guards, remove this poor
man!

Father. O pity! mercy! (Fainting is removed by
guards.)

Hamilton. Such a sight! such a fearful scene!

St. Clair. A happy thought strikes me! Might we
not save Andre still? Bid this old man visit Clinton;
he may move him to surrender Arnold.

All. True, true! Give us that traitor, and we
return the spy!

Wash. Guard! (Enter *Jameson.*) How is the old man? has he recovered?

Jameson. He has, General, and seems calmer.

Wash. Bid him enter. (Exit.) We may yet save Andre.

Father. (Enters supported by guards.) Why recall me? I am calmer now, but I fear it is the calmness which precedes death. What do you want?

Wash. Your prayers would move stones. Here is a passport to New York. You may yet influence Clinton to give up Arnold.

Father. A ray of hope again appears. I will go to them; upon my knees beg them to save my child! If I fail, (glaring wildly around), *I will kill them both!* Yes! (furiously), *they* are the murderers of my child! *They* are his betrayers! I will save him or *die re-venged!* (Exit R.)

All. May you succeed and free your son!

(*Curtain.*)

ACT IV.

SCENE I.—*Hotel in New York, as in Act I.*

Clinton. (Alone.) What a misfortune! Andre in the hands of the rebels; Arnold's papers and mine in that rascal Washington's power! All my plans, my fondest hopes, vanish like the morning fog. And my promises to England! Already all was preparing for a grand celebration at the downfall of the Colonies. Now all will be changed! Lord Germain will be disappointed; the King displeased; the people exasperated; and I may be removed,—disgraced.

O this accursed strife! What misery, suffering, and sad disappointments has it not caused to England's sons? France, I dearly hoped, would be duped, humbled; yet now it will assist our enemy with renewed zest. I thought to win by intrigue, by bribery. I did win Arnold, but even three beggarly fellows, in want of the very necessaries of life, spurned every bribe, laughed to scorn every promise!

The last I heard was, *Andre is condemned to death.* To death? Will Washington not heed my threats of direst vengeance? He seems to be a man of iron, surrounded by hearts true as gold. I sent him a last appeal. What answer will he give? I threatened all that could frighten any man, if Andre is not released. Will he heed my menaces? (Enter *Page.*)

Page. A courier brings this note; he awaits your answer.

5

Clinton. (Hurriedly opening and reading.) "If you deliver Benedict Arnold into our hands, you shall have Andre; if not, Andre dies to-morrow.

"WASHINGTON AND HIS GENERALS."

Infernal rascals! You brave *my* power then! You brave England's wrathful vengeance! Wait, I will make you yield! Tell my generals to meet me here at once.

Page. What answer shall I give to the bearer of this note?

Clinton. I will tell you in time; bid him remain and wait for further orders. (Exit *Page.*) I hate these rebels, yet *must* admire their firmness. I know Major Andre deserves death by hanging. I know that, by delivering him to me unpunished, Washington would sacrifice the honor of the Colonies. But what of that? They are fanatics! They have been, and must *remain* England's slaves! (Enter *Knyphausen, Carleton* and *Graves.*) Welcome, my trusty men! Hear! Washington refuses to return Andre, except Benedict Arnold be surrendered! Shall we conform to his desires?

Knyp. No! By St. George, never! Washington and his bandits are rogues and traitors themselves! How dare they ask us to surrender one who, pressed by his sense of right, has returned to the allegiance he owes England's King?

Graves. No, we cannot, dare not make such terms. We have spent thousands of pounds in trying to bribe these fellows, officers of the army as well as members of Congress; if they once discover that we will give them back when demanded, no matter under what circumstances, our bribes will go for nought. No, we cannot give up Arnold. Will they accept no other terms?

Clinton. None! They are obstinate as demons! Oh! could I but get Washington, or that dare-devil Putnam into my hands!

Carleton. What my comrades have said is indeed true; but, methinks England needs not *bribery* to gain her ends. I hope I offend none, when I express my sorrow that this lamentable affair was permitted to go so far.

Clinton. (Angrily.) Did you not give it your approval? Did you not say it pleased you?

Knyp. Certainly he did! Had it succeeded, he would have shared the glory, now it failed, he shirks the blame. Is that honest?

Carlcton. (Quietly.) One who sells his blood for gold, should not speak of honesty.

Knyp. Dare you allude to me in such terms? I serve my King! He is more my countryman than yours! Remember!

Clinton. (Impatient.) Cease this useless war of words! Shall we surrender Arnold?

Knyp. and *Graves.* No, no, never! It would dishonor England!

Carleton. I say yes, *yes* and *soon!* It will save the innocent!

Clinton. (Furiously.) No! *Lord Clinton says never!* Can I stultify myself so much? I sent Andre, and can I now sacrifice the man who would have gained an easy victory for England, by one bold, fearless

52   MAJOR JOHN ANDRE.

stroke? Arnold shall *never* be surrendered! Ho!
(Enter *Page*.) Give this to the courier; tell him to
hasten to Washington's camp and deliver this last
letter. (Exit.)

Knyp. Mean, low minds cannot comprehend a duty
when it costs something to perform it. Did not Arnold
relinquish his position as Major General in the rebel
army? and for what?

Carleton. For *money!*

Clinton. Colonel Carleton, if any more such expres-
sions are used here, I will order you under arrest!

Knyp. Yes, Arnold is brave! He is self-sacrificing;
not sparing even his——

Carleton. *Honor*, if ever he had that article.

Clinton. Guards! (*Page* enters hurriedly.)

Page. A letter from Washington—of greatest importance, courier says.

Clinton. (Quickly opening and reading.) What,
Andre to be hanged to-morrow! An English noble-
man, and General in his Majesty's army to be hanged
like a dog! By Heavens; it shall not be! Knyphausen, command your army to move at once! (*Robertson*
rushes in—very excited.)

Robertson. Oh, oh! fearful, terrible!

Clinton. In the name of wonder, what is the matter
now? Speak, you idiot!

Robertson. The French and Colonial troops have
landed in great force on the opposite side. The English navy has been driven back—three ships of war
captured and as many sunk. A courier from Lord
Cornwallis says, Gates has gathered together a large
army with which he has retaken Savannah, and is

driving Cornwallis through Georgia.   Everywhere re-
inforcements are necessary.   The city may soon be
bombarded!

Clinton.   Destruction!   Outwitted, defeated at every
point!   To your commands!   We move to-night!
Follow me!

SCENE II.

(*Clinton* about to rush out, is met by *Andre's* father—
all fall back somewhat frightened.)

Father.   Where is Lord Clinton?

Clinton.   Who is it asks for me?

Father.   The wronged father of Major Andre.   Clinton, save my son!

Clinton.   Save your son?   How?   On every side
troops are required to drive back the rebels and their
allies!——

Father.   No soldiers are needed, noble Lord!   I
come from the American camp—he is condemned to
death—to the *gibbet!*   Nothing can save him but the
surrender of Benedict Arnold!

Clinton.   What? surrender Arnold?

Father. Yes, in mercy!   My son was enticed to take
the steps he did.   In mercy to an old, broken-hearted
father, save his son!.   Andre is an Englishman, ready
to sacrifice his life in England's cause.   He has done
even more—he has engaged in unjust means to serve
his country.   Arnold battled long against England;
he now betrays his countrymen from love of money!
Choose between them, and save my boy!

   3*

Clinton. What you require is impossible. I encouraged Arnold to take these steps.

Father. But *he* proposed it—*he* is more guilty! (On his knees.) My Lord, behold an old man on his knees before you! He begs the life of his child! Oh! do not refuse! Oh! hear and grant my prayer!

Clinton. (Unmoved.) Arise old man! Do not trouble *me* with your importunities. Go thy way! If I can liberate Major Andre by honest means, I will; if not—let him die!

Father. (Enraged.) What! let him die! *You* are his *murderer!* You knew the fearful danger he ran! You were his commander; why propose such a foul crime to him? You knew he was brave and would risk everything to serve his King! You knew he was young—the blood ran rapidly in his youthful veins! You, sir, are the murderer of my child!

Clinton. Guards! away with this old wretch!

Father. (Furiously grasping his sword.) You wronged me! You now treat me like a beggar! (Rushing at him—wounds his left arm—fence.) Die! murderer of my child!

Clinton. Keep him off! hold the old villain! (*Knyphausen* and *Graves* hold him—*Clinton* wounded drops sword—staggering back.) Oh! the old tiger wounded me! Take him out; put him in irons! My God! I am dying—help! (Falls into the arms of two guards, who remove him.)

Father. (Still resisting.) Let me go men! You know not a fond father's heart! Oh! mine bleeds for my son! (They take him off—return immediately.)

Robert. It never rains but it pours! Andre captured and about to be hanged; our army and navy everywhere repulsed! Now Lord Clinton himself wounded, perhaps mortally! What may come next?

Carleton. And all for this *traitor Arnold!* Had Clinton attended to his duty properly, instead of arranging matters with traitors, all would have gone well. Now, here we are. No one knows what to do! (*Page* enters.)

Page. Lord Clinton bids you remain here; he is not seriously wounded and will rejoin you in a few moments. The surgeon is now bandaging his injured arm. (Fxit.)

Graves. How dark everything looks for our cause! I pitied the poor old man; his sufferings make his reason totter on its throne! I could not imprison him. Oh! would this unfortunate affair were at an end! (Re-enter *Clinton*, arm in sling, assisted by two guards —sits.)

Knyp. My Lord, I am glad to see you are not severely wounded. Pardon the old man, he is almost crazed by grief.

Carleton. Thanks to that vile traitor Arnold.

Scene III.

(*Arnold* enters in haste.)

Arnold. Lord Clinton, I am here. Like bloodhounds the infuriated Putnam and Knox sought my destruction. I am now at your command. My commission, sent through the unfortunate Andre, I hold. *Revenge* urges me on!

Carleton. (Aside.) Base villain—infamous traitor!

Clinton. General Arnold, give me your hand. See, I am wounded! Andre's father is desperate, and sought my life, because I would not consent to deliver you up to Washington.

Arnold. Noble sir, I thank you! Your magnanimous soul could not descend so low as thus betray the confidence of one who trusted in you. I am not ungrateful! Give me but the opportunity! (Becoming furious.) Washington and his infernal allies, the papist French, desire my life! Ah, I will yet reek a terrible revenge upon them! I will devastate their lands, burn their dwellings, show no quarter! My heart laughs at the terrible ruin I will cause! Where rich fields now greet the eye, desolation shall reign supreme. Where lovely cottages now shelter the wives and children of villainous rebels, smouldering ruins will meet the gaze, and send their ranking smoke to heaven! Yes, I'll have *revenge!* Neither man nor beast shall find mercy at my hands. They call me *traitor;* they may call me *demon*, for like a demon, let loose from the abyss of darkness, I will treat them! My delight shall be to see their ruin! Their groans of pain, their cries of anguish, will be *music to my* ears! I'll taunt them when death's dark agony disfigures their faces! I'll——

Carleton. Infernal demon, shameless traitor, hold thy abandoned tongue, or (drawing his sword) I'll thrust my sword through thy black heart, and stain its bright edge with the blood of a villain, whose presence on God's earth must shame the sun!

Arnold. (Astonished—enraged.) Who calls me villain? What, Lord Clinton, is *this* the treatment I am to expect from your men? (Drawing his sword.)

Clinton. Sheath your swords! Why quarrel among ourselves? Our enemies would rejoice to hear of such brawls!

Carleton. I here and now resign my commission in his Majesty's army. I will not fight side by side with such a demon-hearted rogue!

Arnold. (Furiously.) Take back those words, or I will make them choke you at the point of my sword!

Clinton. Friends, hold!

Carleton. Eat my words? No! Thou art a black-hearted, diabolical villain—a cowardly traitor! Face me! Dogs should feed upon thy carcass rather than an English sword be bedaubed with thy profligate blood! Come on!

Arnold. Am I thus provoked? Then, scoundrel, meet your fate! (They rush upon each other. *Clinton* calls guards. *Knyphausen, Graves, Robertson,* and guards interfere. Curtain falls midst the greatest turmoil and confusion.)

ACT V.

SCENE I.—*Prison.*

Andre. (Alone. Feet chained to the floor. Very sorrowful.) Here I am in chains! The sentence of death, an ignominious death too, lies before me. For months it has been before my eyes, but before the sun seeks the western skies again, I shall be no more! And what a death! To hang by the neck till I am dead! This too in a few hours! Were my end a soldier's death, some little consolation might be left. But no! Like a *murderer*, a *base felon*, I must end my days! O death, death! terrible destroyer, fierce monster! How often have I not spoken lightly of *thee*, braved THEE too when the fight was hottest! Ah, all this was talk or excitement.

What a dreadful night the last of my life! I dreamt I was in England, at home. I was again a child. The loved hand of my mother was softly laid in my plump, boyish hands. I heard her mellow voice sing tones so soft, so sweet, so clear. She kissed my throbbing forehead, and bade me glad good night. Then I was on the commons—fond brothers and dear school companions around me; we talked of deeds of valor, whilst chasing the flying ball, or resting beneath the great elm tree. These youthful visions passed away, and I saw my father. His once stately form was bent by years and sorrow. He looked at me in anger, and demanded why his dearest boy had become a *spy!* Great God! how my heart ached! But, thank heaven, he knows not my sad fate. I will be spared the worst, the greatest sorrow, to see the gray hairs of my father disheveled, his eyes fountains of tears, his whole body a wreck, mercilessly beaten by the waves of suffering. But more I saw. Methought I was standing on the verge of a fathomless deep. Below, all was dark and unknown—they called it the land of the dead! Death! this cannot be the end of my existence. No! there *is* something beyond. My body may be borne to the grave, but my spirit must endure forever. How is it I never thought of *this* earnestly before? Strange feelings surround one when at the point of death!

This life cannot have been the end of my creation; it was too short, too transitory! The bright star of hope, of success, rose in my horizon a few years ago, and already has it set. Was I created for this? It cannot be—it would be mockery! Why then have others not taught me my true and only end? I went to England's best military schools and learned to fence, march and manœuvre; to advance, retreat and ambuscade; to command an army; but *nothing* was taught me of a higher life! *What a dreadful cheat is education without* GOD! My poor parents, this night in my dark and dreary dungeon, death before me, I almost cursed you for teaching me so little of *God*, of *Eternity*, of *Heaven*, of *Hell!* Could I but live, with what joy would I learn to know God, to love and serve Him! With what care would I search for truth, with what happiness embrace it! Alas, alas! my life has been an empty farce! Much of this world have I learned, but little of the future! It is so hard to die so young, youth's blood coursing swiftly through my veins, but

harder still because I feel my life has been vain.
(Kneeling.) O God! pity my ignorance, and have
mercy on my poor soul! I repent of every unjust act
and would gladly make any amends required of me.
(Rises—silent for a moment.) In youth I used to
laugh when I saw the papist steal into the confessional;
but even then, his glad face when the task was done,
surprised me and made me wonder. Yet I heard
nothing but evil of the Romish Church. Woe to
those who taught me to think evil of it, if after all, it
is the Church of God! But why do these strange
thoughts torment me now? Is it my troubled fancy,
or is it perhaps the last ray of grace which the angel
of salvation brings me before I die? Oh! how cruel
doubt, dark uncertainty, wring my heart! This too,
when time for me is no more! My brain swims—O
peace! Troubled soul thou longest for rest and peace!
(Sits down, burying his face in his hands.)

SCENE II.

Andre's Father. (From without.) Have pity on
an old man! Unhand me, I must see him!

Andre. (In greatest agitation.) My God, that
voice! I know that voice! Oh, my cup of sorrow
is filled to overflowing!

Father. Oh God, my son! (Together, falling
Andre. My father, dearest father! in each other's arms—a momentary silence.)

Father. (Still clinging to *Andre.*) Oh, is it thus I
find you! a prisoner in clanking chains! O dearest
boy! your cruel fate breaks your father's heart!

Andre. Calm yourself, dear father. (Aside.) My heart, my heart, cease! How calm my father when untold woe overcomes me!

Father. Is there no spark of hope? Tell me you may yet be saved!

Andre. Be calm and try to soothe your grief; there may yet be deliverance. I sent a last appeal yesterday, but have no answer from Lord Clinton yet. He may still find means to save my life.

Father. (Disengaging himself—steps back.) Alas! my boy, you have not acted strictly honest. England needs not *traitors' swords* nor *spies* to win her victories.

Andre. Father, such words from your loved lips! Rebuke me not! I consented before considering the nature of the act. I looked but to the danger.

Father. (Warmly.) I know my boy, you are honest and were misled by those who should have guarded your enthusiasm.

Andre. Lord Clinton was ever kind to me.

Father. (Enraged.) Speak not of that dog, Clinton! He is the murderer of my child! He could save you now, but will not! On my knees I begged him! like a worm, I dragged my old bones upon the floor before him! He ordered menials to remove me as you would remove the carcass of a dog! Then fury overcame me! I grasped my sword and rushed on him, and he may now be dead, for I thrust it at his black heart! You die not unavenged, my son!

Andre. O father! what have you done! Lord Clinton's death, if he die, will be your ruin. You too will perish on the gallows, a murderer! O horrible!

6

Father. Say an avenger, child! There is another whom I owe a debt of blood: that vile knave, dark villain, nameless traitor, Arnold! (Drawing sword.) Would my sword you could luxuriate in his heart's blood! But dread vengeance will yet overtake him ! A broken-hearted father's curses will follow him like raging demons through the wide world. May evil meet him at every step ! May the furies of darkness surround him by night, and the avenger's dagger glitter before his eyes by day! May his drink be potations of fire; his meat, the poison of asps ! May—

Andre. Father, father, be quiet, be calm! your dreadful imprecations frighten me!

Father. (Solemnly.) Ah, *traitor !* I see thee wandering an exile, hated, detested, shunned! England's children despise thee; those thou wouldst betray execrate thee! In want and misery, the demon of starvation at thy door, black despair hovering over thee, scorned, cursed, thou wilt end thy worthless life !

Andre. Oh, be silent of them, father ! Tell me of my mother, brothers and sister! Do they know my sad fate ?

Father. (Sorrow-stricken.) Know? yes, all England knows! Your mother's eyes are red with weeping! Her sunken cheek, distracted look and faltering step, show too clearly that the means of your death have reached and broken your mother's heart! She prays for you, but, alas ! 'tis the prayer of despair.

Andre. O my mother! dearest, best of mothers! (Weeps.)

Father. Your brothers, too, are buried in sorrow, but the fire gleaming from their eyes, speaks of vengeance! Marie, the sweet little elf, can only cry because she sees her mother weep.

Andre. Oh, father, father, cease! you unman me! I hear steps. (Aside.) How quick the time has flown! the hour arrives! (Aloud.) Father dearest, leave me now. I would be alone. (Aside.) I must conceal from him the worst!

SCENE III.

(Enter Talmage.)

Talmage. I am sorry, sir, to inform you——

Father. (Looking towards the door at which *Talmage* entered—horrified—wildly.) What is that? What is that? A gallows! for whom, for whom?

Andre. (To *Talmage*.) I know all. Go, shut that door! (Exit.)

Father. (Following—increasing excitement.) See! see! the gallows! Are they for you? My son, are they for you?

Andre. (Drawing him away.) Come away, father, come! Go now, you are too excited! Be calm, be quiet! (Aside.) O Heavens! yes, they are for me!

Father. What! leave you now, when I see you at death's door? No, I will not! O my brain! The gallows! (Raving.) The terrible gallows! Are you a dog that they should hang you? No, never, never! I will die before I see you hanged! The gallows! Come, let us fly!

Andre. Father, be quiet, we cannot fly! (Aside.) O horror! his reason wonders! Mercy, my God! have mercy on my father!

Father. (Raving more wildly.) The gallows! Hang my boy! Escape! Cut down (drawing sword) yon guard! Oh, oh, my brain! Escape! See, see, that demon! That serpent strikes his fangs deep into my son's heart! Fly, fly! Back, murderer, back! See his burning eyes! fire flashes from his nostrils! Back! help!—away—O mercy! (Staggers—falls, exhausted.)

Andre. (In despair.) My poor father! Guards, help! my father is dying! Help, for mercy, help!

Talmage. Great Heavens! what is the matter? what has happened?

Andre. Oh, in mercy, water—wine! He still breathes! (Exit *Talmage.*) Alas! what misery, what suffering! My poor, dear father! how must you love me!

Talmage. (Returning.) Here is a glass of wine it will revive the poor old man. (Assists *Andre.*)

Andre. (Forcing the wine on his *Father.*) Oh, may it help him. (*Father* opening his eyes.) See, see! he lives, he breathes! Father, dearest father, I am still with you!

Father. (Suddenly arises—stares wildly around.) Where am I? who are you? (Exit *Talmage.*) Ha, ha! (hoarse, maniacal laugh,) they told me my son would be hanged! Ha, ha, ha! what sport! Let me go to America! I will see him hang!

Andre. (Horrified.) A maniac! Oh, has it come to this! My poor heart! My dear father a raving madman!

Father. (Staggering wildly around—flourishing his sword.) Come, the war dance! Join in! All hands!

Hurrah ! The gallows are ready ! Ha, ha! wake up ! they will hang my son !

Andre. (Clinging to his father.) Father, father ! Listen to me, hear me.

Father. (More wildly.) Come on ! Join hands ! Here goes ! Put the rope on his neck ! Pull now ! Ha, ha, ha ! (Falls heavily.)

Andre. (Weeping.) Guards, help ! (Enter *Jameson* and *Talmage.*) Oh, he is dead ! My father, is this your farewell ! Must I thus leave, loved one, thus leave you ! A maniac—died a maniac ! (Guards remove him—*Andre* keeping hold of his hands as long as he can.) Now this life has lost everything worth living for ! Would the hangman might come and free me ! I now long for death, as once I longed to live !

SCENE IV.

(Enter two guards, taking their stations on *Andre's* right and left—*General Putnam,* accompanied by *Parsons* and *Colonel Clinton.*

Putnam. (Solemnly.) Major John Andre, the hour has arrived. Hear thy death warrant. (Reads very slowly.) "Major John Andre, you have been found guilty, upon your own confession, of the crime of being a spy. This crime is punished with death. We condemn you to die, the execution to take place at 8.30 A. M., on the second day of October, in the year of our Lord, one thousand seven hundred and eighty. May God have mercy on your soul.

"GEORGE WASHINGTON, *for the Commission.*"

6*

Andre. (Boldly.) I am ready.

Putnam. If you have anything more to say before you die, say it now.

Andre. I have a last request to make. Give my body to Lord Clinton, with my money and other articles of value.

Putnam. We shall do so gladly.

Andre. Another word. I fear not death; to me it is a deliverer; but I beg to die a soldier's death!

Putnam. This I cannot grant.

Andre. Then tell the world I died as became a brave man! (Guards unloosen his feet, and put the handcuffs on his hands.) To *hang!* The thought is horrible—but it's only a momentary pang, and all is over.

Putnam. Forward! (Enter two drummers with drums draped and muffled—March off very slowly in the following order: drummers; *General Putnam* with drawn sword; *Andre* between two guards; *Parsons* and *Clinton.*)

Music: Dead March.

<h2 style="text-align:center;">Scene V.</h2>

(Enter *Lafayette, Washington* and *Hamilton,* sorrowfully observing the train from the stage.)

Hamilton. See how bravely he meets his death!

Lafayette. He does not falter! Look, his face grows pale at the sight of the gallows! But it changes—it was but the feeling of honest shame to die such an ignominious death!

Wash. God knows how gladly we would have spared him this last disgrace, but we could not, and preserve our country's honor. It pains me to the heart to see one so young, so noble, die such a death.

Hamilton. History will never censure you; only Clinton and Arnold.

Lafayette. See, they have arrived at the gallows! He mounts with a firm, unfaltering step! The black cap is drawn over his face! They are counting the seconds! (Shot heard.) All is over!

Hamilton. Never man died so justly, and deserved death so little!

(*Curtain.*)

TABLEAU. *Music:* " Peace, troubled soul."

N B.—The following Tableau is suggested by the writer. It was presented on two occasions at the College, and always received with the greatest applause.

Major Andre and Father in front centre—dead—heads resting on a black pillow—Andre's face covered.

Washington in back centre—U. S. Flag in one hand —sword in the other pointing to the flag—*Hamilton* pointing towards Andre and Father, on his right—*Lafayette* pointing towards Arnold, on his left.

Arnold in left corner—back—as if fleeing in despair.

Clinton—left front—arms folded—very sorrowful.

Knyphausen, Robertson and Graves on Clinton's right.

Colonel Carleton—right front, one hand extended towards Clinton, the other towards Arnold—very stern.

American Officers on the right—swords pointed towards Arnold—very angry, &c.

Paulding, Van Wert and Williams, with *Smith* in their midst, between Washington and the English officers.

Page—weeping over Andre.

Light up with *red* fire.

THE END.

www.ingramcontent.com/pod-product-compliance
Lightning Source LLC
Chambersburg PA
CBHW022150020726
47496CB00008B/2651